S0-AMO-391

The Golden Touch

A Retelling of the Legend of King Midas

Written by **Glen Huser**

Illustrated by **Philippe Béha**

Music by **Giannis Georgantelis**

TRADEWIND BOOKS

Vancouver ••London

Have you ever made a wish

and when that wish came true
It turned out that someone must have played a trick on you?
It turned out that someone must have played a trick on you?
A wish that you might wait up for a fireworks display
Only to nod off and sleep the time away?
A wish that you could have a pet to call your own
To end up on your birthday with a fancy painted stone?
A wish that on the playground, kids would notice you,
But not for falling down and turning black and blue?

A wish, a wish, a wish, a wish, a wish . . .
Tricky wishes—watch for them!
Be careful what you say.
Fate may have a wish itself
To simply ruin your day.
Tricky wishes—be on guard!
Watch the words you choose.
Wish-givers can be jokers
And you're the one to lose.

Have you ever made a wish—only then to find
What you get's quite different from what you had in mind?
What you get's quite different from what you had in mind?
A wish that you'd miss school and take a trip downtown,
To end up in a dentist chair nearly upside down?
A wish to take a ride on a lofty Ferris wheel,
And at the very top, upchuck your latest meal?
A wish your angling gear might snag a weighty prize—
But it's a rubber boot that your fishing hook supplies!

A wish, a wish, a wish, a wish, a wish . . .
Tricky wishes—watch for them!
Be careful what you say.
Fate may have a wish itself
To simply ruin your day.
Tricky wishes—be on guard!
Watch the words you choose.
Wish-givers can be jokers—
And you're the one to lose.

Close your eyes for a minute and imagine a time when gods and men shared the wonders of the world—along with creatures that were half human. If you were travelling through the woods, you might come upon a band of fauns who sported the bodies of men but the legs and hoofed feet of goats. And if you spotted one with grey hair and a beard carrying an armful of scrolled texts along with his jug of wine, that would be Silenus, a schoolmaster—who is only wise half of the time.

You might guess that the younger fauns who should have been at their studies have been leading him on. And you would be right.

Tip your jug, Silenus—
We've worked enough today.
It's time for fun and frolic,
To dance and drink and play.
We've had enough geometry
And political debate;
The dialogues of Plato
Are thick and overweight.

Tip your jug, Silenus—
We'd sooner tear around
And wake the local wildlife
With a joyful boyful sound!

Play the pipes and frolic—
We're boys just out for fun.
Pour the wine and pluck the lyre—
The dance has just begun.
La la la la la la la . . .

Tip your jug, Silenus—
Drink the last drop down.
It's time to celebrate
And let all sorrows drown.
Don't tell us of the gods
And the tragedies they face,
Who has angered Zeus
And who is in disgrace.
Tell us of the tricksters—
We want to laugh, not cry.
Tickle us with stories—
A laugh will satisfy!

Play the pipes and frolic—
We're boys just out for fun.
Pour the wine and pluck the lyre—
The dance has just begun.
La la la la la la la . . .

When Silenus was through spinning stories and had emptied his jug, his goat-footed students pranced away into the woods. The old faun noticed that the world was wobbling around him. He moved unsteadily from tree trunk to tree trunk until he came to a rose garden at the edge of the wood. A mossy mound in the middle of the garden took on the sudden appeal of a soft bed. Silenus staggered over and fell into a deep sleep, his scrolls scattered around him.

Imagine the next morning, Helios in his chariot guiding the sun so it warms the old faun still curled up and snoring. It brings a blush to the petals of the many roses in bloom. But whose garden is this? Do you see that bearded man with the odd crown on his head and garden shears in his hands out for a morning stroll?

I am the King of Phrygia; a crown is on my head—
But where I am the happiest is here in my rose bed.
Instead of a royal sceptre, I have my garden shears,
And there's no one 'round to laugh at my hairy donkey ears.

Instead of a royal sceptre, he has his garden shears,
And there's no one 'round to laugh at his hairy donkey ears.

They say Apollo's vengeance is why my ears are long
Because I made him runner up—and chose another's song.
But in my garden I say, "Pooh!"—I couldn't give a fig—
Roses really couldn't care whose ears are small or big.

I am the king of Phrygia; I rule and I command—
Yet my people often snigger and laugh behind a hand.
But here amongst my roses, I know I've got respect—
Flowers are very gracious and always circumspect.

Here amongst his roses, he knows he has respect—
Flowers are very gracious and always circumspect.

I am the King of Phrygia; a crown is on my head—
But where I am the happiest is here in my rose bed.
I am the king of Phrygia; I rule and I command—
Yet my people often snigger and laugh behind a hand.

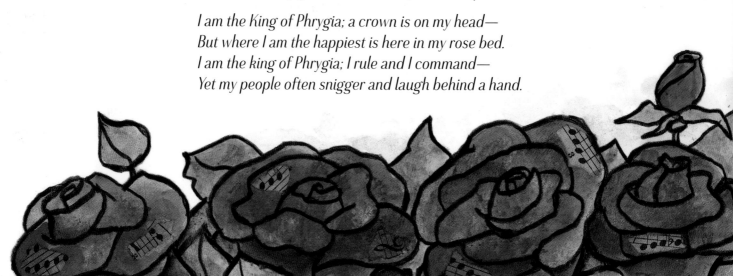

As Midas looked up at the morning sun and scratched his ears, he stumbled over something in the middle of his rose garden.

It groaned, sat up and rubbed its eyes. "Is that you, Midas?"

"Cousin Silenus!" Midas could not believe his eyes. "What are you doing here, sleeping in my garden?"

"I'm not sure. I must have got lost."

"Won't Dionysus be looking for you?"

Silenus rubbed his eyes again. "Midas, where did you get those floppy ears?"

"A gift from Apollo." The king sighed and tucked them up into his crown.

Silenus burst out laughing and shook his head. "I hope my master, Dionysus, doesn't honour me with a gift like that."

"Come." Midas smiled and offered Silenus a hand up. "You must rest at my palace. Wait there until Dionysus comes to fetch you. The queen will not hear of you heading off without a good visit."

But Midas knew that wasn't true. His wife had no love for this side of his family.

The queen was furious. "I've told you a million times not to bring your drunken goat-footed relatives here."

Midas ducked as a vase whizzed by his head and crashed into the wall.

"Now, my dear, don't be hasty. Dionysus will be looking for Silenus. The last time he went missing, Dionysus paid a generous reward for his return. He may offer gold."

"I don't care if he offers us the universe!" the queen shrieked.

At that moment their daughter, Princess Zoe, bounded into the room.

"Who's offering the universe?" She laughed.

"Your mother was joking." Midas hugged Zoe. He loved his daughter more than anything, even more than his roses. "We have a special guest staying with us."

"Who?"

"Silenus. He's a wonderful storyteller. When I was a child, we gathered at his knee to hear the amazing tales he told."

"Stories! I love stories."

"Then you must ask him to tell us some after our evening meal."

That evening—and for many of the evenings that followed—
Silenus charmed the royal family and their dinner guests with
tales that caught the first flickers of candlelight and lasted until
dawn streaked an early morning sky.

Tell us a story, Silenus, spin us a tale of old,
Words that you gift us, Silenus, are better than treasures of gold.

Listen while I tell you of a Cyclops I once met—
A one-eyed monster you're not likely to forget.
Living next to him was something you'd avert—
Since he often ate a neighbour or two for his dessert.

Did I tell you of the gorgon, the fierce Euryale?
Yes, an immortal with reptilian pedigree.
If you locked eyes with her, that snake-headed crone,
Before you knew it, friend, you'd be turned into stone.

Tell us a story, Silenus, spin us a tale of old . . .

Sit back and harken to a tale of Ancient Troy,
Of pretty Princess Helen and her handsome loverboy.
And how their love affair really went off course
When the enemy constructed a hollow wooden horse.

Well, how about Charybdis, a monster of the sea—
A specialist in witchcraft and ocean thuggery?
She'd watch out for sailboats adrift upon the tide—
Then whip up a whirlpool and suck them down inside.

Tell us a story, Silenus, spin us a tale of old . . .

After Silenus had been in the palace for
ten days, the god Dionysus came looking
for his old schoolmaster.

"Midas!" he exclaimed when he saw
how well Silenus looked. "I can't
thank you enough for caring for
my dear old friend. He's never
looked more hale or hearty.
Your kindness is deserving of a
gift—so ask away. Anything you want."

"Let me think about it," Midas said.
While Dionysus was generous, he knew
the god was also something of a trickster.
It would be best to consider carefully what
to wish for—and how to word the wish.

Midas rushed to tell the queen of
Dionysus' offer.

See, my dear, I told you—it was good to bide our time.
We can garner enough gold to last our whole lifetime.
Golden gates and galleys, gold jewellery to wear—
Gold sandals on your feet and gold hairpins in your hair.

Don't be stupid, Midas—don't wish for something rash.
Think that we'll get pleasure from a lot of golden cash?
You might wish to be a poet with words that always rhyme—
Or wish you had a voice—like Orpheus—sublime.

Don't be a donkey, husband—don't be so obtuse—
You might consider something that I would find of use.
Wish for me great beauty—so all will turn and stare
At Midas and his wife—that queen beyond compare.

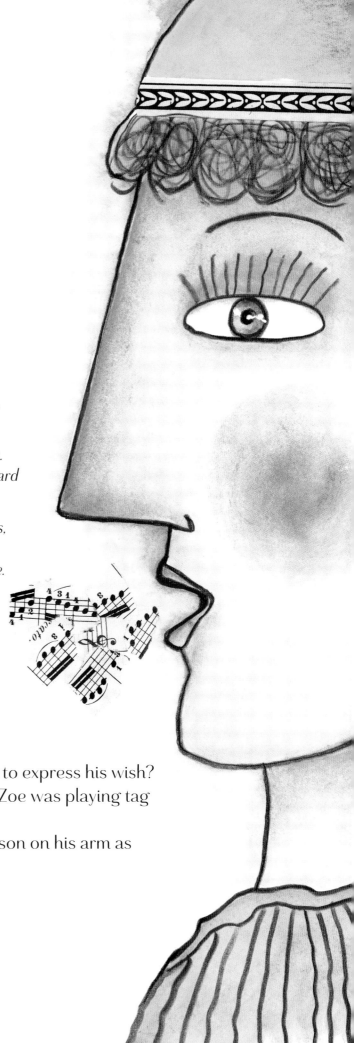

Gold, gold, gold, I'm weary of hearing that refrain.
But think of wealth and power and all we can attain!
Gold, gold, gold, I love it—I think I hate it now.
Love it! Hate it!
Gold! But what to say!
I just need to find a way—I wonder how?
I wonder how?

Oh fudge and fiddlesticks—beauty soon is gone,
But piles of golden treasure, live on and on and on.
Gold will give us comfort in our golden, senior years.
Gold to run our hands through when all else disappears.

Fiddlesticks yourself, you king of all milquetoasts—
You might wish for a physique like the god Apollo boasts.
You could have a chiselled chin, and muscles firm and hard
Instead of looking like a great big tub of lard.

And most of all you might, to stop those laughs and jeers,
Wish to rid yourself of those loathsome donkey ears.
Your barber and crown-maker may help with their disguise.
But they are always present in everybody's eyes.

Don't say another word. Tub of lard indeed!
Just because I failed to keep that diet you decreed.
You'd best, my dear, accept that I have a bit of fat,
For I shall ask for gold and that's the end of that.

Gold, gold, gold, I'm weary of hearing that refrain . . .

What was the best, the perfect way in which to express his wish?
He paused at a hall window and looked out. Zoe was playing tag
with some of her friends.

"You're it!" she cried, touching the baker's son on his arm as
she ran past him.

Eureka! Midas thought. That's the answer.

The king found Dionysus helping Silenus gather his scrolls for
his trip home.

   "So, Midas, have you thought of a good wish?"

   "Yes, but I hesitate to ask—"

   "Anything, Midas. Silenus and I are most grateful."

   "Then grant that anything I touch will turn to gold."

   Midas didn't notice the knowing glance that passed between
the god and the old faun.

   "You're certain? A wish once granted cannot be revoked."
This wasn't exactly true. It was simply something Dionysus
preferred not to do.

   "Yes," Midas repeated. "Anything I touch—"

   "Granted, then." Dionysus smiled and passed his hand over
the king's crown.

They had barely been gone a minute when Midas began dancing about, waving his fingers in the air. Such a wonderful gift! What would he touch first? He thought of the beautiful roses in his garden and his sandals were soon flying over the paving stones that led there.

There was an especially beautiful blossom that he had been cultivating. Now he reached out and touched it. At once the blossom turned to pure gold, dazzling in the sunlight.

Midas plucked it and bore it back to the palace.

"Darling," he called out to his wife. "I have something to give you."

The queen was in the dining hall, checking that everything was ready for their midday meal.

"Look—pure gold. For you." As he reached over to give the rose to her, his hand brushed against a tray of fruit. In an instant the entire tray turned to solid gold—gold apples, gold pomegranates, gold grapes.

"What have you done!" the queen shrieked.

"It's my touch," Midas said. "Anything I touch will turn to gold. Imagine—"

"Well, don't touch me." His wife glared at him. "And don't touch any more of the food."

Midas paused. He had a sinking feeling. He nodded to one of the servants. "Pour me some wine."

As he picked up the goblet, it turned to gold and the wine inside the cup also turned into hard gold. He reached for a piece of bread and it, too, turned into the solid metal.

Great Zeus preserve us!
What will Midas do? (Oh no!)
Where will his fingers land
In his golden wish debut?
Follow in his footsteps
But never stray too close
Unless you want to end up
Like crusty golden toast.
Unless you want to end up
Like crusty golden toast.

Great Zeus preserve us!
He leaves the dining hall. (Oh no!)
The cat he pets becomes
A golden hard hairball.
He wanders by the laundry
And touches, unaware—
He's turned his favourite gonches
Into metal underwear!
He's turned his favourite gonches
Into metal underwear!

Great Zeus preserve us!
He tries to keep hands free, (Oh no!)
But the guard by the gate
Is now gold filigree.
And what's he doing now?
Picking up a scroll?
See it drop upon the ground
Creating a pothole.
See it drop upon the ground
Creating a pothole.

"Dionysus tricked me after all." Midas sobbed as he blundered into the courtyard. Blinded by his tears, he grasped the edge of a fountain, which turned at once to gold. The water bubbling from it hardened and became silent.

Zoe was returning from playing tag with her friends, when she saw her father and his distress. She ran over to him and before he could stop her, grabbed his hand.

"No!" Midas' cry echoed over the palace grounds.

The queen came running out. "Zoe!" she screamed in horror, and
then turned on her husband. "You monster! See what you've done
to your only child!"

    Midas ran his hands over Zoe's stone-hard curls, her cheeks
and lips of solid gold. And then he turned and ran, through the
rose garden and into the solitude of the woods.

> *What have I done! I'm such a fool—*
> *Gold's made of me a slave.*
> *I've lost my child, my love, my world—*
> *And gold will be my grave.*

I touch a tree, a willow tree;
The leaves shine bright and cold—
A startled blackbird flies away
From brittle branches gold.

He wanders in the woods alone.
He leaves a trail of gold
And thinks about his darling child
He can no longer hold.

He wanders in the woods alone.
He holds himself to blame
And weeps for his sweet child—Zoe—
Who will never be the same.

Let me wander in the woods alone.
Creatures small can watch me weep—
Hard gold grass, my forest bed,
Where I shall have no sleep.

I touch a tree, a willow tree . . .

He wanders in the woods alone . . .

In the forest, the schoolmaster's band of fauns was searching for Silenus. They had been scolded soundly by Dionysus and told not to return until they found him. Being sons of Pan, they were finding it difficult to keep their minds on what they were supposed to be doing. Poimenios, who hated any exercise except dancing, complained loudly.

How many days has this search gone on—
Trying to find that old wandering faun?
We've combed through caves and checked behind stones,
Listening for snores or the creak of his bones.

We've not had a break since Helios rose.
I'm so very weary—I'm almost comatose.
Ampelos and Gemon, Leno and Lycoon—
Bring out your pipes and play us a tune.

With your echoing pan notes, materialize
The image of maidens with dark sparkling eyes.
We'll rest as we listen—spin a daydream—
Pan pipes and bird calls, a rippling stream . . .

Pan pipes and bird calls . . . we only need wine
To make this search party completely divine.
Lamis, Orestes, unpack the food—
Bring out those lamb chops that you have barbecued.

La la la la la la . . .

Dolmades we'll nibble; whistles we'll wet,
Humming along with our pan-pipe quartet.
And when we are all completely refreshed,
We'll search for Silenus, continue our quest.

La la la la la la . . .

By the time they had dined and drunk their fill and had an afternoon
snooze, there was not much left of the day. Poimenios was already
thinking it might be time to head home. There was always tomorrow.

That's when Ampelos spotted something very unusual. Helios was riding low in the sky but his rays were being caught on something just beyond them, through the trees, that glittered and flashed. The fauns hurried through the woods to see what it was. They were amazed to find a willow tree, its leaves and branches all turned to gold.

But it was not Silenus who crouched mournfully at its base. It was Midas, the chubby king who ruled in the land just beyond the woods.

"Have you seen Silenus?" Ampelos asked.

"Don't come near me. If I touch you," Midas moaned, "you will be frozen in gold. Your teacher, Silenus, has been found—and this was my reward!"

The fauns kept a safe distance as Midas told them his tale of woe.

"Dionysus says a wish once granted cannot be revoked. So I am doomed. And my daughter is doomed." Midas sobbed.

The fauns looked at one another. They knew that Dionysus, when he was feeling good—and that was most of the time—could be persuaded to change his mind.

"There may be some hope for you," said Lamis.

"Follow us," urged Poimenios, "but stay well behind."

"None of us want to be turned into gold," said Ampelos, laughing.

When they reached Dionysus' palace, the fauns left Midas outside and then hurried in to find the god.

There's a very sorry king in a very sorry state—
Standing, filled with sorrow, beside the garden gate.
He wants to beg your mercy and pleads that you reverse
The golden gift you gave him that's become a wretched curse.

Midas, King of Fools, the world ridicules
The thought that gold will bring him happiness.
Midas, King of Fools, destiny unspools
An end that's filled with sorrow and distress.

There's a very sorry king and he fears you won't relent
And take back the wish so terribly misspent.
He's turned his little girl into something dead and cold—
His regrets have multiplied at least a thousandfold.

Midas, King of Fools, the world ridicules
The thought that gold will bring him happiness.
Midas, King of Fools, destiny unspools
An end that's filled with sorrow and distress.

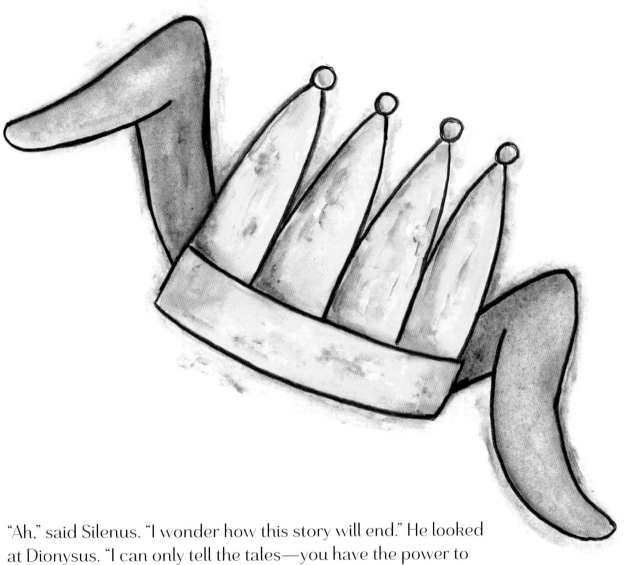

"Ah," said Silenus. "I wonder how this story will end." He looked at Dionysus. "I can only tell the tales—you have the power to shape them."

"True." Dionysus rubbed his chin thoughtfully, then smiled and rose from his dinner table. Everyone followed him outside. Midas stood there trembling, afraid to move.

"The fauns have told me of your troubles." Dionysus shook his head. "You've brought this disaster on yourself, but today the sun is shining, the music is sweet—and so I cannot bear that anyone in my presence be so gloomy. I know of a way you can rid yourself of your golden touch."

"Oh, please," Midas begged, "anything. I'll do anything you ask."

"Follow me to the river Pactolus. Wash yourself there and all the dreadful effects of your silly wish will disappear."

As Midas was making the journey to the river, the queen continued to mourn her lost daughter. She stayed in the garden, unable to leave the statue of Zoe.

Who would believe that I would have to grieve
For a daughter alive and laughing yesterday.
Gold she's become—gold of eye and gold of thumb—
Just some heavy hulking metal to display.

Pardon me while I stop, and find a good dust-mop—
I'm dusting off my daughter, can't you see?
I'm polishing her nose, sweeping off her toes—
Very sad work for a mother, you'll agree.

I'm shooing off the flies, while saying my goodbyes
To the child that I used to tuck in bed.
If that pigeon should drop, and leave a pigeon plop—
The bird will soon be resting with the dead.

I'm wiping off the bugs and the trails of garden slugs—
On the statue of my daughter once so dear.
It is a very good thing that my husband—Midas, king—
Is hiding out a long way off from here.

Midas was more weary than he had ever been when they reached the river Pactolus. A crowd from the countryside, curious to see this strange parade of fauns and a god with a king in tow, gathered on the banks.

"Wade into the water," said Dionysus. "Immerse yourself."

Midas did as he was told. He felt soothed by the rippling current, as if the weight of the world was washing away from him.

Those watching on the bank gasped. They could see spirals of gold shimmering away from the king into the water and settling into the sands.

"Know this to be a river of golden treasure," Dionysus announced. "Mine its banks and sands. Those whose labour is honest and true will be rewarded."

When Midas crawled out of the river, he cautiously touched a bulrush growing on the bank. It remained green and bent slightly in the gentle breeze.

Midas leapt to his feet and embraced Dionysus.

"Thank you! Thank you!" he cried. "Tell me, is my daughter—?"

Dionysus nodded.

At the same moment that her husband was wading into the river Pactolus, the queen had finished cleaning and polishing the garden statue that Zoe had become. Her fingers trailed sadly over one of Zoe's arms.

The gold felt softer than it had a minute ago.

She touched the arm again.

Could it be? Yes, the gold was draining away! Life was returning to Zoe's limbs, her hands, her face. The queen wrapped her arms around the statue, weeping as she felt her return to life.

"What's the matter?" A puzzled Zoe looked up into her mother's face. "Why are you crying?"

"You were lost, my darling," the queen sighed. "But now you're home again."

Mother, oh Mother, I've had the strangest dream—
I was lost and wandering beside a golden stream.
Helios in his chariot, waved at me below
And all the world around me took on a golden glow.
And by that sparkling river, upon a sandy shoal,
Silenus sat writing some words upon a scroll.
And when I wandered over, he smiled up at me,
Said, "Look at you, my dear, in your golden finery!
You're dressed for your part in a story to be told
About a greedy king who turned his daughter into gold.
You will live forever, when people tell the tale
Of how, inside a wish, lay the seed of a betrayal."

Zoe, you were sleeping—
The world held its breath
And hoped you would awaken
From that golden death.

Stories I love—but I felt that I might cry—
For I'd be the girl who would turn to gold and die.
And so I tried to run and leave Silenus there—
But I couldn't move and I was gasping out for air.
On gold dust I was choking—I wanted to scream
But no sound came out . . .

. . . oh sweet, it's just a dream.
You're here, alive and breathing, and warm within my arms,
You have a lifetime waiting—the world will know your charms.
You'll find love, raise a family, and in time—grow old,
And that will be a treasure, dear, much better far than gold.

Zoe, you were sleeping—
The world that held its breath
Now celebrates your waking
From that golden death.

It was many hours before Midas was able to get back to his palace. But when he got there, everyone was waiting for him. The guardsmen and the servants cheered. Zoe ran forward, laughing and clapping her hands.

"You'll never guess what happened to me!" she said.

Midas hugged his daughter, and sighed as he caught a glimpse of his wife's forgiving smile.

Coming home to find you
Alive and waiting here
I know the real gold
Is all that I hold dear.
Yes, my queen—and daughter,
The people of my land,
I've left behind my folly
In Pactolus' sand.
Coming home, I greet you,
Embrace you fearlessly—
And hope we'll flourish
One and all,
*   And all remain gold-free!*

It is gone now—that time when gods and men shared the wonders of the world along with creatures that were half human. That world where Midas, briefly, had his wish come true and held the dreadful gift of a golden touch.

And yet there is a golden touch, a magic at work, that we have only to open our eyes and see.

Throughout the world, there's evidence we see
Of golden treasure shining in nature's gallery.

Gold the sun that rises and shines throughout the day,
Gold the fields of grain and stacks of bundled hay,
Gold the buttercup, reflections in a stream,
And in a darkened attic, a straying gold sunbeam.
Gold the tiny fish that glitter in a tank,
Gold the tawny coat of a palomino's flank,
Yes, we can be thankful, thankful for so much—
For that wonderful, mysterious, amazing golden touch.

Gold the petals of an April daffodil,
Gold the dandelions upon a distant hill,
Hammered gold the moon within a midnight sky,
Gold the outspread wings of a sulphur butterfly,
Gold the warming glow that issues round the wick
Of a candle burning brightly in a golden candlestick.
Yes, we can be thankful, thankful for so much—
For that wonderful, mysterious, amazing golden touch.

Gold the feathers of a tiny finch in flight,
Gold the glittering stars in the canopy of night,
Gold the shining leaves of an October tree,
Gold the bristled coat of a busy honeybee,
Dusty goldenrod, and marigolds in bloom,
Gold of flickering fireflies in the evening gloom.

Yes, we can be thankful, thankful for so much—
For that wonderful, mysterious, amazing golden touch!

Yes, we can be thankful, thankful for so much—
For that wonderful, mysterious, amazing golden touch!

Glen Huser is the recipient of the Governor General's Award for Children's Literature and is the author of many highly praised novels for young readers. He lives in Vancouver, BC.

One of Canada's preeminent illustrators, **Philippe Béha** is a two-time winner of the Governor General's Award. He has illustrated over 180 books for children. He lives in Quebec.

Giannis Georgantelis has composed music for theatrical plays, multimedia projects and festivals, as well as musical ensembles. He lives in Athens, Greece.

Chroma Musika and **Panarmonia Atelier Musical** (DEKA 2010 & NEPMCC awards) were founded by Greek-Canadian opera singers and recipients of the Medal of the National Assembly of Quebec, Maria Diamantis and Dimitris Ilias. Their work has promoted high quality music activities for Canadian children, families, local communities as well as the general public. Their discography includes two CDs and five children's operas with accompanying picture books and CDs. Maria and Dimitris live in Montreal.

AUDIO CD

Cast

NARRATOR
Terry Jones

THE QUEEN
Maria Diamantis

MIDAS
Dimitris Ilias

SILENUS
Desmond Byrne

PRINCESS ZOE
Juliana Theodoropoulos

POIMENIOS
Nicholas Mouteros

DIONYSUS
Desmond Byrne

AMPELOS & LAMIS
Tristan Kalmbach

TARANTELLA SINGERS
Alessia Marie
Laura Leone-Bernabei
Georgia Kanellopoulos
Julia Scuccimarri
Sabrina Lima
Sophia Kotsiopoulos
Alessia Marie Pietraroia

WOODLAND SPIRIT
Eve Prévost

Production

MUSIC/ ORCHESTRATION
Giannis Georgantelis

MUSICAL PRODUCTION
Chroma Musika & Panarmonia Atelier Musical

EDUCATIONAL DIRECTION
Panarmonia Atelier Musical

MUSICAL AND VOCAL DIRECTION
Maria Diamantis & Dimitris Ilias

ORCHESTRAL SCORE
Giannis Georgantelis

ASSOCIATE MUSIC DIRECTORS
Andrée Beauséjour
Céline Sévigny
Elaine Thomas
Elizabeth Lefebvre
Nancy Bennett
Samantha Sobol
Shawna Dunbar
Susan Cunningham
Stefania Lancione
Justine Dansereau

VOICE OVER & ACTING COACH
Susan Bain

ASSOCIATE VOCAL DIRECTOR
Marialena Spinoula

SCORE CORRECTIONS
Stavros Katirtzoglou

CHORAL COORDINATOR
Patricia Regan

THURSDAY REHEARSAL COORDINATOR
Jacinthe Vezeau

SUPPLEMENTARY MUSICAL DIRECTION
Tip your Jug: Andrée Beauséjour, Elizabeth Lefebre
Zoe's Song and Silenus Ballad: Céline Sévigny

RECORDING-MIXING OF ORCHESTRA AND CHORUS
Dr. Mark Corwin (Montreal)

RECORDING OF TERRY JONES
Andre Jacquemin-Redwood Studios (London)

RECORDING OF SOLOISTS
Dimitris Ilias-Chroma Musika (Montreal)

FINAL MIX - MASTERING
Kostas Parisis-Studio Praxis (Athens)

RECORDING LOCATIONS
Redwood Studios (London)
Studio Praxis (Athens)
Oscar Peterson Concert Hall (Montreal)
Chroma Musika (Montreal)
Mother Teresa Junior Auditorium (Laval)

Choirs

The Sir Wilfrid Laurier School Board Youth Chorus

Arundel: Brayden Lamadeleine, Chanelle Boisvert, Malyk Eli Jean Baptiste, Rebecca Puddifer, Amber Vary, Olivia Tremblay, Sarah Anne Charlebois **Crestview:** Julia Ruccolo, Samantha Maslia, Savanna Campbell Brown, Aidan Konovalenko, Aliya Billeter, Bianca Pereira, Evanthia Theofanis, Jenika Albert, Sevana Aynejian **Franklin Hill:** Ella Mottillo, Benjamin-Taylor Sauve, Jennifer Delicato, Laura Leone-Bernabei, Sabrina Lima **Genesis:** Ashazia Dussault, Jordane Belanger, Liana Bourque, Frédérique Guénette, Liana Lombardi, Olivia Caruso, Sofia Solomita, Christian Dussault, Olivia Bourque **Grenville:** Sadie Ethel Gauthier, Amy-lee Lapointe, Gregory Foreman, Mia Goulet-Martini, Hannah Pearson, Hannah Trineer, Faith Campbell, Megan McCart, Michaela McCart **Hillcrest Academy:** Emmanuela Mecca, Marina Tsagaris, Saige Shrier, Alexandra Floyd, Alexandra Pavlatos, Constantina Moraitis , Francesca Maruta-Paternostro, John Peter Tsagaris, Lea Briglio, Lia Masi, Sofia Rodrigue, Emma Aquino, Evagelia Rokas, Shreya Dev, John Fotinos **John F. Kennedy:** Anastasia Kokkinos, Giulia Conte, Diego-Michael Sanscartier, Iman Janjua, Rushil Kumar Godavathi, Ryan Azimov, Bianca Beldie, Elie-Sami Cyr **Joliette:** Sabrina Richer **Lake of Two Mountains:** Kayla Lorraine Carlino **Laurentian:** Elyse Robert, Cameron Ross **Laval Junior:** Anna Maria Lerga, Dahlia Thibodeau, Darcy Sumsion, Katrina Morillas, Liliane Grenon, Nicholas Mouteros, Nikeisha Larin Joseph, Praise Omogbai, Vivienne Zikos, Zeina Hage Kaplo **Laval Liberty:** Eveshore Omogbai, Jenny Kordos, Juliana Theodoropoulos, Kristina Pouliezos McCaig: Maya Frayret, Melina Guevremont, Téa Frayret, Ciera MacDavid, Zoé Frayret **Morin Heights:** Anita Jade Turcotte, Natalia Lore Secor-Friedman, Romy Juliana Secor-Friedman, Sophia Clark, Angie Rowat, Juliette Beaudry, Mia Rose Lauzon, Reese Boutin, Kaelyn Hodge **Mother Teresa Junior:** Brianna Grace Scalia, Evangelos Vavinis, Myriam Sauvageau **Mountainview:** Michael Rozza, Rosemary Comeau, Sienna Bergeron, Mackenzie Leigh Carlino, Mickaëlla Hardy, Maya Nagy, Sarah Ayotte, Emma Steben **Our Lady of Peace:** Laura Manzano, Mara Kanellopoulos, Robert Edvi, Ashley Malone, Brienna Fraser, Tyler Holbis, Esha Joshi, Georgia Kanellopoulos, Stephanie Nicole Pabst-Leonidas **Pierre Elliot Trudeau:** Michael Chouliotis **Rosemere:** Adrianna Chouliotis, Melina Mailhot **Saint Vincent-Concord Centre:** Annabella Armenti, Ema-Sofia Andricciola, Gemma Dufresne, Giulia Rosato, Kassandra Chery, Siena Rosato, Alexandra Maria Aubé, Kiara Picone, Alessia DiMenna, Alessia Marie Pietraroia, Allicia Ouimet, Clara Smythe. Éloïse Fréchette, Gabriella Rubbo, Kayla Sousa, Laurie-Anne Lefebvre, Kassandra Rodrigue, Liana Corsetto, Valeria Mastrangelo **Souvenir:** Anna Asselin, Juliana Marz, Christina Alacchi, Meghan Greco, Serina Parmar, Ageliki Kasidiari, Amelie Melki, Franco Fiovo Gagliano, Georgia Pappas, Irene Nikolidakis, Kostadina Katsifolis, Maria Chandris, Evangelos Tzortzis, Spyridon Tzortzis **St Jude:** Alexia Tolias, Antonio Maraventano, Brianna Fasoli, Evan Ménard, Lea Larichellière, Angelica D'Éramo, Caleb Lampron, Jade Desjardins, Cassidy Grande, Chloë Jobba-Lawton, Dylan Lunny, Eve Prévost, Summer Klimas, Sylina Lunny, Tiara Malik **St Paul:** Maia Theresa Marino, Sina-Madison Galvano, **Ste-Adele:** Isaïe Skeye Bernatchez **Terry Fox:** Jérémy Turmel, Jade Chaumette St Louis, Jennifer Niro, Samantha Niro, Sofia De Fazio, Tristan Skeete, Jana Hage-Kaplo, Patrick Sauvageau, Pietro Calderone, Angelica DeLuca, Marie-Angeles Mercedes Boccardi **Twin Oaks:** Tristan Joseph Drescher, Ana-Maria Bérubé, Anne-Sophie Gélinas, Luca David Parnas-Zver, Maxime-Terrence Mali, Olivia Rose Bonfa, Renee-Maria Makdessi, Sarah-Jane B Beaumier, Trinity Jade Lambrakis, Catherine Tremblay, Emily Bertrand-Oliver, Mikalia Lekakis, Sophia Kotsiopoulos

CHORAL SOLOISTS
Éloïse Fréchette, Valeria Mastrangelo, Gabriella Rubbo, Alessia Marie Pietraroia, Lea Larichellière

SUPPLEMENTARY RECORDING SOLOISTS
Alexia Tolias, Evan Ménard, Angelica D'Éramo, Brianna Fasoli, Antonio Maraventano, Jade Desjardins, Lea Larichellière, Siona Nazarian, Nafsika Baloukas, Georgia Baloukas

AUDIO CD

The Orchestre Symphonique Pop de Montréal

CONDUCTOR
Alain Cazes
FIRST VIOLINS
Julie Lapierre (violin solo / Concertmaster), **Nadine Guénette, Anne-Isabelle Bourdon, Veronica Tamburro, Larisa Mak Mak**
SECOND VIOLINS
Bulard, Tim S. Savard, Katarzyna Fraj, Joyce Blond Frank
VIOLAS
Caroline Neault, Jennie Ferris, Heather Weinreb
CELLOS
Dmitry Babich, Nicolas Cousineau, Juliette Lees
DOUBLE BASSES
Nicolas Belpaire, Blake Eaton
FLUTES
Michelle Moreau, Myrtha Boily (Piccolo)
CLARINET
Emmanuelle Guay Da Silva
OBOE
Emily Burt
BASSOON
Danielle Hébert
FRENCH HORNS
Guillaume Hétu, Sarah Joyal
TRUMPETS
Francis Leduc Bélanger, Mireille Tardif
TROMBONES
Alain Talbot, Olivier Lizotte (Bass)
TUBA
Benjamin Joncas
HARP
Suzanne Berthiaume
PIANO
Hélène Carrière
TIMPANI
Lanny Levine
PERCUSSION
Stéphane Savaria (Batterie / Drumset), **Martin-Paul Beaulieu, Julien Bodart**
MUSIC LIBRARIAN
Caroline Neault

FOUNDER AND CEO
Stéphane Savaria
VICE-PRESIDENT & TECHNICAL DIRECTOR
Hugues Morissette
ASSISTANT VICE-PRESIDENT
Geneviève Lanouette
ASSISTANT TREASURER
Hélène Bellemare

Musicians - Athens

ACCORDION, PERCUSSION AND SYNTHESIZER, SOUND EFFECTS
Giannis Georgantelis

MUSIC GROUP CAROUSEL (TARANTELLA)
ACCORDION
Giannis Georgantelis
ACC. GUITAR & PERCUSSION
Makis Papagavriil
FLUTE & PICCOLO
Fotis Mylonas
ELECTRIC BASS
Apostolos Kaltsas
GUITAR
Stavros Katirtzoglou

VOCALS ON THE DEMO RECORDINGS
Marialena Spinoula, Makis Papagavriil and Feni Noussia (Carousel)

Chroma Musika and Panarmonia Atelier Musical wish to thank the following sponsors, partners and individuals for their immense support.

The city of Laval

La Corporation des célébrations 2015 à Laval
Ce livreCD a été publié grâce à la contribution financière de la Corporation des célébrations 2015 à Laval dans le cadre des projets citoyens.

Partners

The Sir Wilfrid Laurier School Board
The Sir Wilfrid Laurier Foundation
Bombardier Inc.

Sponsors

DIAMOND CIRCLE
Embassy Plaza banquet and conference center
Laval Families Magazine

PLATINUM CIRCLE
Hon. Guy Ouellette (MNA for Chomedey)
Freeman Audiovisual Canada
Les productions sixdegreesinmotion (Official videographer)
Photogenia Studio (Official photographer)
Olivier Larichelliere (website)

GOLD CIRCLE
The Hon. Saul Polo (MNA for Laval-des-Rapides)
The Hon. Jean Rouselle (MNA for Vimont)
Société de transport de Laval
Le Smart Burger
Ousia Cuisine Grecque
Micca Paint /Peinture Micca- Patrick Rodrigue – director of operations

HOSPITALITY SPONSORS
Restaurant Elounda – Bobby Michailidis
Joey's Limousine – Joey Fumo & Christina Maroudas
Anikó Pelikán – Personal Chef

Media Partners

The Greek-Canadian News (TA NEA)**, Park-Ex News, Laval News, CFMB 1280 AM Radio Montreal, Laval Families Magazine**

Government Liaisons

Senator Leo Housakos, Hon. Guy Ouellette (MNA for Chomedey), **David De Cotis** (City Councillor and VP of the exec. com. City of Laval)

Under the Auspices of:

The Government of Canada, The Government of Quebec, and The City of Laval

Sir Wilfrid Laurier School Board

Jennifer Maccarone – Chairperson
Stephanie Vucko – Director General
Tina Korb – Director of Educational Services
Geoffrey Hipps – Assistant Director of Educational Services

Special Thanks to:

Senator Leo Housakos, the Hon. Guy Ouellette (MNA for Chomedey),The Hon. Christine St-Pierre, The Hon. Gilles Ouimet, Christine Long (CTV News), Morgan Dunlop (CBC News), Luigi Morabito, Angelo Amicone, George Guzmas, Sept Frères Construction G2 Inc., Claudia del Balso, Adria Trafficante, Annik Dupras, Barbara Imbrogno, Bruna Casagrande, Cathy Stilianesi, Effie Kontakos, Ekaterini Karalis, Elizabeth Michailidis, Felitsa Tsakiris, Gianvita Bonaduce, Glynis Devine, Jacinthe Vezeau, Jack Fasoli, Joanna Donas, Kathy , Kirkey, Kathy Lariviere, Kellie Drouin, Kristine Mouteros, Laurie Modugno, Linda Beach, Litsa Babalis, Lucia Alicandro, Maria Bardouniotis, Mary Zver, Michelle Goulet, Nadine Hage, Nancy Lubert, Nina Ciancio, Panagiota (Peggy) Sarantopoulos, Patricia Ayotte, Patricia D'Aliesio, Louise Robineau, Renee Legault, Rolande Villeneuve, Stamatia Gazetas (Toula), Tina Bergeron, Tino Masi, Carmen Maruta, France Medaino, Dena Chronopoulos, Tracy Barrie, Stephane Brunet, the Ilias & Diamantis families and all the families of our young songbirds for their dedication.

The Golden Touch

CD Tracks

Published by Tradewind Books in 2015. Text copyright © 2015 Glen Huser. Illustrations copyright © 2015 Philippe Béha. Music copyright © Chroma Musika & Giannis Georgantelis. All rights reserved. No part of this publication or CD may be reproduced, stored in a retrieval system or transmitted, in any form or by any means, without the prior written permission of the publisher or, in the case of photocopying or other reprographic copying, a license from Access Copyright, Toronto, Ontario. The right of Glen Huser, Philippe Béha and Giannis Georgantelis to be identified as the author, the illustrator and composer of this work has been asserted by them in accordance with the Copyright, Design and Patents Act 1988.

Book design by Elisa Gutiérrez

The type is set in Grenale. Title type is Honeydukes.

10 9 8 7 6 5 4 3 2 1

Printed and bound in Korea in August 2015 by Sung In Printing Company.

The publisher wishes to thank Elsa Delacretaz for her French translation of the text. The publisher also wishes to thank Olga Lenczewska and Ayushi Nayak for their editorial assistance.

. . . .

LIBRARY AND ARCHIVES CANADA CATALOGUING IN PUBLICATION

Huser, Glen, 1943-, author
     The golden touch / Glen Huser ; illustrated by Philippe Béha ; music by Giannis Georgantelis.

(Children's opera series)
Text to be accompanied by a compact disc of the musical work, composed by Giannis Georgantelis (story and lyrics by Glen Huser), narrated by Terry Jones.
ISBN 978-1-896580-73-9 (bound)

     1. Midas (Legendary character)--Juvenile fiction. 2. Operas--Juvenile--Librettos. I. Béha, Philippe, illustrator II. Georgantelis, Giannis, composer III. Jones, Terry, 1942-, narrator IV. Title. V. Series: Children's opera series

ML50.H969G62 2015   j782.1026'8   C2015-903078-1

. . . .

The publisher thanks the Government of Canada and Canadian Heritage for their financial support through the Canada Council for the Arts, the Canada Book Fund and Livres Canada Books. The publisher also thanks the Government of the Province of British Columbia for the financial support it has given through the Book Publishing Tax Credit program and the British Columbia Arts Council.

 Canada Council **Conseil des Arts**
for the Arts **du Canada**

 BRITISH COLUMBIA ARTS COUNCIL